By the same author and illustrator
MY MUM AND OUR DAD

VIKING
Published by the Penguin Group
Penguin Books Ltd, 27 Wrights Lane, London W8 5TZ, England
Penguin Books USA Inc. 375 Hudson Street, New York, New York 10014, USA
Penguin Books Australia Ltd, Ringwood, Victoria, Australia
Penguin Books Canada Ltd, 2801 John Street, Markham, Ontario, Canada L3R 1B4
Penguin Books (NZ) Ltd, 182-190 Wairau Road, Auckland 10, New Zealand

Penguin Books Ltd, Registered Offices: Harmondsworth, Middlesex, England

First published 1992
10 9 8 7 6 5 4 3 2 1

Text copyright © Rose Impey, 1991
Illustrations copyright © Maureen Galvani, 1991

The moral right of the author and illustrator has been asserted

Set in Monotype PostScript 18/22pt Times New Roman Schoolbook
Printed in China by Imago

A CIP catalogue record for this book is available from the British Library

ISBN 0-670-82857-2

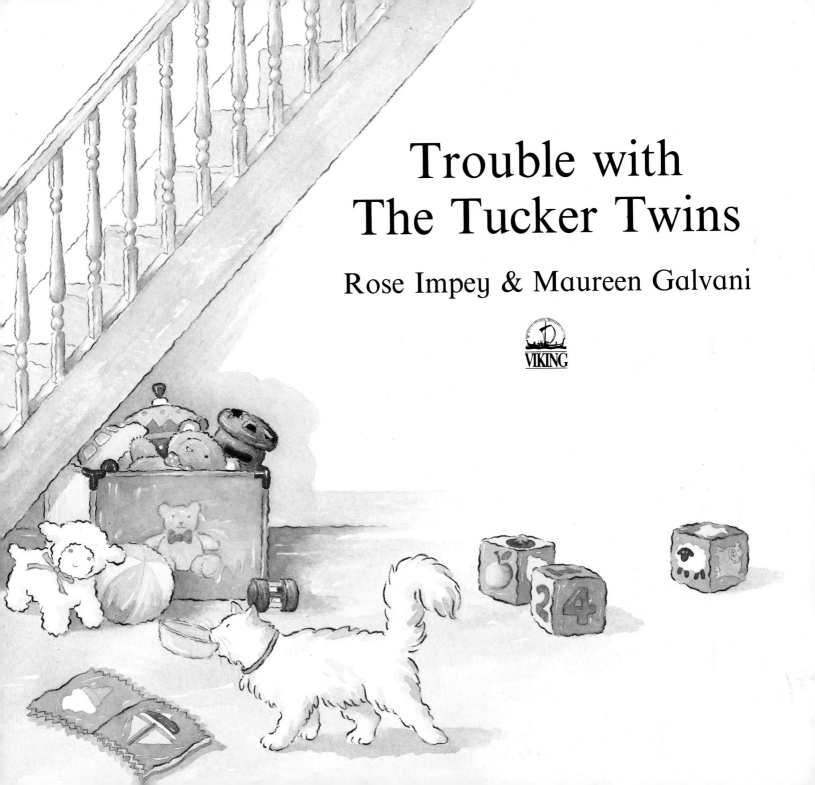

Trouble with
The Tucker Twins

Rose Impey & Maureen Galvani

VIKING

Mick didn't want to get up.

He said he felt poorly.

"Where does it hurt?" asked Mum.

"Here...and here...and...everywhere!" said Mick.

Mick's mum said,
"I thought you liked school."
"I do like school," said Mick,

"but I don't like the Tucker Twins."

The Tucker Twins sat at Mick's table.
They weren't very tall
and they weren't very tough,
but the trouble was...
there were two of them.

Wherever Mick went...

the Tucker Twins were there.

They pinched Mick's things.

They ate Mick's sweets.

When it was boiled fish for dinner,
they put *their* left-overs on Mick's plate.

And once they made Mick keep a slug in his glove for a whole day.

"I'm sick of them," said Mick.
"Well," said Mum, "hiding in bed
won't make the Tucker Twins disappear."
"I wish something would," said Mick.
"You could put a spell on them," said Mum.
"That wouldn't work," said Mick.

"How about a little disguise?"
"Don't be silly," said Mick.

"A suit of armour?"
"No," said Mick. "Definitely not."

"Did you tell the teacher?" Mum asked.
But Mick shook his head.
So Mum told Mick a secret.
"You know even bullies are soft inside."
"Not the Tucker Twins," said Mick.

At breakfast Mick wasn't very hungry.
He tapped on his egg,
but it wouldn't crack.

"Just like the Tucker Twins," said Mum,
"hard on the outside, soft inside.
Now *tuck* into that."
Mick began to laugh.

When Mick got to school,
he saw one of the twins in the playground.
Mick held on to his hat and his scarf.
He hid his crisps.
But the Tucker Twin didn't even notice.

After PE, when he couldn't tie his laces,
the Tucker Twin burst into tears.

At playtime, when he fell off the climbing-frame, the Tucker Twin burst into tears.

And at lunch-time, when it was boiled fish again, the Tucker Twin burst into tears.

In the afternoon,
when he couldn't do his sums,
Tony Tucker said,
"I want to go home."

"What's wrong?" asked Mick.
"Don't you like school?"
"I don't like it without Tom,"
said Tony Tucker.
And tears fell
on his number book.

He wasn't very tall
and he wasn't very tough
and now there was only one of him.
So Mick said, "I'll show you how to do it.

At home time Mick and Tony Tucker
walked to the gates together.
When Tony saw his mum and Tom waiting for him,
he burst into tears...again!

And then...so did Tom!

As they walked home from school
Mum asked, "Well, what did you learn today, Mick?"
And Mick said:

"Even **The Tucker Twins** are soft inside."